© 1992 The Walt Disney Company
No portion of this book may be reproduced
without the written consent of The Walt Disney Company.
Produced by The Creative Spark
San Clemente, California
Illustrated by Yakovetic Productions
Written by M.C. Varley
Printed in the United States of America.
ISBN 1-56326-152-9

Flounder's Folly

One morning, while the Little Mermaid and her friend Flounder were playing on a calm, blue sea, they saw three ships sailing off in the distance. "Humans!" cried Ariel excitedly. "I wonder where they're going?"

"On an adventure!" Flounder replied. "Someday, I'm going to go on an adventure, too!"

"Someday, Flounder," Ariel said, "but not now. You're just too young to go exploring."

"I am not!" Flounder pouted. "I'm old enough! And I'd be really careful!"

Ariel hadn't meant to hurt her little friend's feelings. "One day, Flounder," she explained, "the whole world will be yours to explore. But you'll just have to wait until you get bigger."

But that wasn't what Flounder wanted to hear. "Nobody ever lets me have fun," he pouted as he swam back under the sea.

"What's that I hear you complaining about?" asked Sebastian the crab. "Not having any fun? And just whose fault is that?"

"It's Ariel's fault," the little fish complained. "I want to go exploring, but she says I have to hang around this dumb old island until I'm older."

"She's right, you know," Sebastian said. "You might get lost, and we wouldn't want that, would we?"

"I wouldn't get lost!" Flounder protested. "Why can't anyone see I'm old enough to have an adventure on my own?"

An adventure, thought Sebastian. *That gives me an idea.*

The next day Sebastian called his friends together in the lagoon. "All right, everyone, it's time for an adventure!" he said. "I've hidden a prize somewhere around the island. I'll give you a clue: It's a very thorny problem, but when you find the prize, success will smell very sweet. Now, let's see who can find the prize."

"That's a wonderful idea!" said Ariel.

"Simply grand," agreed Scuttle.

"Neat," said Scales.

"Flounder, what do you think of our adventure?" Sebastian asked.

But the little fish was nowhere in sight.

"What a stupid idea," Flounder whined as he swam away from the lagoon. "It's not like a real adventure at all." Just then he spotted one of the ships he and Ariel had seen the day before. "They can play their dumb game if they want to," Flounder decided, "but I'm going on a real adventure!"

Flounder swam as fast as he could to catch up with the ship, but it was no use. The ship was just too fast for him. "Wait for me!" he cried, but the humans didn't hear him, and soon they had disappeared over the horizon.

Tired and disappointed, the little fish started to swim back home. But nothing he saw looked familiar to him, and the island was nowhere to be seen.

"Uh-oh," said Flounder. "Which way do I go?"

Meanwhile, Ariel and the others were still looking for the prize. Then Ariel remembered Sebastian's clues. *Let me see, roses have thorns,* the Little Mermaid thought. *And they definitely smell sweet, too.* Sure enough, she was right—Sebastian's prize was hidden in the roses that grew along the island's shore.

Ariel hurried back to the lagoon to show everyone her prize. Her friends all thought she was very clever to have figured out Sebastian's clues. "That leaves just one more puzzle to be solved," said Scales. "Where's Flounder?"

Flounder was lost. And scared. And wishing he were back home with his friends. "Do you know which way home is?" he asked an octopus, but the octopus just shrugged and pointed his eight huge legs in every direction at once.

"Do you know how I can find my way home?" he asked some clams, but they were all asleep in their beds and didn't want to be disturbed.

"Can you help me find my way home?" he asked a school of jellyfish, but jellyfish are never any help at all.

"What will I do now?" the little fish cried. "Sebastian and Ariel were right! I am too small to go exploring!"

Suddenly, all the other fish started swimming away as fast as they could. "Wait!" Flounder shouted. "Where are you all going?" Just then a huge shadow fell over him, and the water grew very cold and still. He knew, even without looking, what everybody was so afraid of. It was a...

SHARK!

Flounder swam as fast as he could as the shark's razor-sharp teeth snapped at his tail. He zigged and he zagged, but the giant jaws kept getting closer and closer and closer. Then, just when the shark was about to catch him, Flounder squeezed through a small opening in a pile of rocks.

While the shark tried to squeeze through the hole on one side, Flounder swam out the other. The little fish didn't stop to look back. He just swam and swam. And before he knew it, he was almost back home! He didn't know how he got there, all he knew was that he would never, ever, EVER go exploring alone again.

"There he is!" cried Sebastian. "There's Flounder!"

Everyone took turns looking through Sebastian's spyglass. They waved and shouted as Flounder swam closer. They were so happy to see that their little friend was safe.

"Where have you been? You had us worried sick!" everyone said when Flounder arrived at the lagoon. "We thought you were lost forever!"

"It was horrible!" Flounder shivered as he told his friends about his adventure. "There was this great big shark with about a million teeth and, oh, I'm so glad to be back home!"

"We're glad you're home, too, Flounder," said Ariel.

"You were right, Ariel," admitted Flounder. "I guess I am too young to go exploring by myself. I should have listened to you. From now on, I'll have all my adventures right here around the island. The rest of the world will have to wait—at least until I'm as big as that shark!"